AF432210

The Mouth

A Short Story by:

Noel Daniels

Eric woke to the sound of Gran's wooden spoon scraping the bottom of the porridge pot, footsteps in the hallway and the unmistakable touch of morning rubbing at the cold tip of his nose. He never felt safer than when he was snuggled deep inside the warm cocoon of his bed. The door creaked inward, the light from the hallway bright to his sleep covered eyes. Gran was saying something, he did not catch the words but the meaning was clear. It was time to face the world, to act, and pretend that he understood. It was time to make the world believe the lies that he told himself. He dressed in silence, powder blue shirt, grey pants, black socks and black shoes polished to a mirror shine, his bottle green blazer fitting snugly over his narrow shoulders. The ensemble was completed by the maroon tie, hideous, like a noose around his neck. Uniformed and ready for school he stepped out of his bedroom.

Eric wondered as he dragged himself to the kitchen, why he could not feel the same way that other people did. Maybe they were lying too and pretending to feel the things that people are supposed to feel. He was so world-weary he hardly lifted his feet as he shuffled on; kitchen bound. When he reached the kitchen table, he propped himself up in a chair like a rag doll. Gran dropped a bowl full of hot porridge in front of him. He stared at it for a long time, becoming increasingly aware of the tik tik tik tik of his mother's perfectly manicured nails as they drummed the table. "Well?" she said pointing with her nose at the white hot tasteless glob that was his breakfast. Eric looked up at her, then, back to the porridge. He was trying to make the connection, straining his thoughts; everything was slow as if he were under water. He heard all that she spoke, the sound of Gran moving about the kitchen filled out the background, but he could not make sense of it, he could not find a connection so he stared at her vaguely.

Eric never felt her hand touch his face. One moment he was seated at the table the next he was laying on the floor. He felt his face getting hot as he realised that Mother must have slapped him. He stood up holding his hand protectively over the burning flesh of his cheek. Somewhere far in the distance he heard her voice, she was yelling at him telling him that he was stupid. Asking why he was so stupid. He heard the dull sound of the porridge bowl as it hit the ground next to him. Mother grabbed his head, and forced him face first into the porridge that lay spread out under the table. What his mother was doing did not seem to bother Eric, which sent her into an ever maddening rage. What bothered him was that Gran just went over to the sink and started to run water. She was doing the dishes! After a few moments Gran came over and retrieved the porridge bowl, wordlessly she carried it over to the sink and proceeded to wash it in the warm soapy water.

After he finished eating his breakfast off the floor like a dog, Mother grabbed his ear and pulled him upright. Gently she undid his pants, tucked his shirt into his underwear, and refastened the clasp of his grey school trousers. She straightened his buttons, smoothed his tie over his chest and then, she stood up and kissed his forehead as if nothing was amiss, "Now… off to school my Angel " she said. Her breath was hot in his ear and he could smell coffee and cigarettes on her, all mixed with her sweet perfume, Chanel Coco Noir, a scent far too heavy and rich for day time use. It was at this point that he noticed she was wearing the same dress from the previous day. He knew it was the same dress because he remembered thinking it was too sexy work time. She returned to her seat and began to drum the table again. Tik tik tik tik…

~~~

Eric opened his eyes. Two lazy wounds that refused to remain closed. He blinked, and as the world came into focus he noticed the gore that dripped from his hands. He was sitting on the edge of a bed, naked, covered in blood, as if he were, newborn to the world.

At his feet he saw a thing, he knew the shape of the thing but he could not figure out what it was that lay there. He looked at it, curious. He knew that he should know this thing, but it was alien to him, far removed and strangely appealing. He sat there for the longest time just staring at the thing. Like him it was covered in blood, and like him it had once been something living.

He must have abandoned the thing at some point, because when his thoughts returned to a normal measured pace he was in the bathroom. Looking at his reflection in the mirror, his face was smeared red, his hair matted to his forehead in locks that appeared dark purple. His eyes black pits against his blood stained skin. His thoughts returned, after a minute he remembered the thing that lay at the base of the bed. The thing was far away now, like a memory.

The walls that lay thick around his sluggish thoughts gave way… Anna-Leigh. It's name was Anna-Leigh. He turned around and padded back to the room, standing at the edge of the bed Eric looked down, the thing had a proper shape now, soft curves that could be the crest of a woman's breast. Dark hair sprawled around a head like a frozen black pool. The longer he looked at it the more it looked like a woman; somewhere in the back of his mind he knew that her name was Anna-Leigh.

His gaze drifted to what he thought could be a face. And then… he saw the eyes, hazel orbs of dead light, like the last embers of a once bright fire. His mouth opened and closed like a fish and then he heard it; a scream, a hoarse sound that seemed to go on forever. In his mind's eye it
~~~

came for him. His mouth folded around itself, backward until it wrapped around the back of his head. From there it moved down his neck, he felt his shoulders crunch inward as the mouth moved further down, to his waist. Then he felt the warm wetness around his hips, slippery it pinned his hands down… further now to his knees… it pulled his shins together… ankles… and then he was gone swallowed up into the warm wet darkness. Just before he gave up to the darkness he stifled a giggle as the taste of copper became ever stronger.

Eric was in the dark place now, but he could see everything around him. It was as if the light had been sucked out of the world yet he felt that he could see more. It seemed to Eric that he could see through things. From where he stood he could see his reflection in the mirror and he could see Anna-Leigh's body. He used to believe that she was the most beautiful creature alive, but now he could see her blemished skin, the split ends of her hair lying in the drying pool of blood. He could hear all the cruel jokes she used to make at his expense. He could see her ears were too large and that it made her look mousey. He could see her thighs were pock marked with cellulite and he could see her left breast was smaller than her right. The room was suddenly very small and dirty, the carpet stained by time and the excretions of former occupants. The walls that had appeared stark white were filled with scratches and age worn dirt. He could see all the dirt of the world, all the filth that lay hidden under the romance of hope. The scales were lifted from his eyes and he could see the beautiful dirt, the glorious perversions of creation.

Looking in the mirror he saw a different version of himself. He was tall like a sculpture made of bronze. He felt his arousal grow as he looked at himself. He was beauty devoid of gender, age or race. He was aesthetics made flesh. Eric stood and marvelled at his own image. He flexed his muscles; his perfect physique responded and he wept at the sight of his own beauty.

~~~

It was cold and heavy clouds hung in the sky but it did not rain. Eric pulled his blazer tight around himself and his wool cap down over his ears. He pushed on as the wind angled in sharper, looking for gaps in his uniform. His feet and hands felt like ice blocks and he turned his head down to protect his eyes from the biting cold wind.
~~~

Eric had just passed Anna's house; he was halfway to school, her house was in the middle of the lane on his right , on his left an open park, with a jungle gym and a slide, all set in concrete at the centre of the muddy square. It was meant to be a play park for toddlers and preschoolers but, reality found it an outdoor drug den. Even now in the biting cold with heavy rain looming a group of maybe seven youths sat huddled together, preparing their pipes. No weather on earth would interrupt the ritual; there were drugs to be smoked and too much time in a day. One of the mob poked his head up like a meerkat as Eric came up level with his party. He shouted over the wail of the wind, calling Eric to join them. Apprehension clutched his heart, and it beat faster. His first thought was to keep walking, as it was, he would already be late for school, but curiosity got the better of him. He changed direction, jumped over the low wood fence that marked the edge of the park and headed toward the group of teens.

The youths were all high school age, but only one of them wore a uniform. Eric recognized him from church but he could not remember his name. He did however remember that he was the son of the Parish Priest. As Eric approached an argument erupted between the Priest's son and the one that had called him over. From what Eric gathered the Priest's son did not want Eric to 'burn the pipe'. He stood in front of the group, and looked from one to the other wondering what they wanted. The one that had called him over held out a broken bottle neck filled with what to Eric looked like grass. Still unsure of what they wanted he just stared at the broken bottle neck; the jagged edges looked cruel in the dim light. The youth told him to take the pipe. Eric reached out and did as instructed. Once he had hold of the pipe the entire group burst out in nervous laughter. They crowded around him, and the laughter died down, one of the group produced a box of matches from his pocket. Eric watched his movements closely, fascination and dread mingled with excitement at being included. He pulled two matches from the box, one was burnt at the tip and one was unused, he turned the burnt end around and held the pair out in his right hand, the match box he held with his left. He struck the match and cupped it, protecting the flame from the wind. Once both matches were burning brightly he held them out to Eric. The entire movement was a practised flurry. "Smoke" a disembodied voice said from somewhere in the huddle.

Eric had never done anything like this before and he was still unsure of exactly what to do. He held the mouth of the bottle neck to his lips, the youth brought the burning matches into position and instinct did the rest. Slowly, deliberately he drew on the pipe until thick acrid smoke filled his mouth and lungs. His eyes filled with tears, his lungs burned and as he blew out the smoke he began to cough. He coughed with his whole body as if his very soul was being pulled out. Again the group laughed, loud and mocking, his pain and confusion a salve to their aching self-loathing. The Laughter died down and an expectant hush settled over the group. The youth with the matches lit a second pair and they bid Eric to smoke again. This time he did not cough. As he handed the pipe back, he noted that a demeanour of respect had settled over the group, his vacant stare was met with a slight nod from each of them in turn. Except for the Priest's son, when Eric met his eyes he averted his gaze. Shame and guilt sat on him like an old winter coat. The one that called Eric over, produced a scrap of folded newspaper. He told Eric that his part was done, and thanked him for his service. The group laughed again. He unfolded the newspaper and Eric could see it contained white powder. As he turned to leave he wondered what the powder was. Walking away he looked over his shoulder and noted that the youth was adding some of the white powder to the pipe, while the mob looked on with earnest faces.

By the time Eric reached the school the drugs clouded his mind like a blanket wrapped warm around his consciousness. His short term and long term memory mingled together forming a strange mind-state. He was present in the moment but the moment felt like a memory. As if he was remembering the experience he was having. He walked through school gates and heard the long siren that indicated classes had started. He was late. Usually he would run when he heard the siren, but not today. It seemed to Eric that it would not matter all that much. Late was late, whether it was very, or not very much.

~~~

Her Body was pale, against the blood spattered sheets. She was surprisingly difficult to lift, and Eric was out of breath as he looked at her from the base of the bed. In life her skin had the healthy bronze hue of the perpetually tanned. She was a beach queen by day and dance queen by night, her life a permanent party. In death she was just ordinary. After her bowels released and the stink of her filled the room she was the ugly thing that Eric saw. She was nothing, her decaying body proof that she was no more than another dead thing.

He stood and marvelled at the sight of her, she was revolting, her body stiff with rigour mortis. It had only been a few hours since Eric had taken the life from her but the humid air and the lack of Air-conditioning in the room was already causing her body to decompose. Her once rosy lips had turned purple. The white of her eyes were bloodshot and turning yellow, her belly bloated
~~~

with gas. Gingerly he climbed onto the bed and crawled over her, sniffing like an animal. Naturally he started at her feet. Moving from one to the other, before he moved up her thigh, when he reached the triangle between her legs the smell was so bad he had to turn his head to gather fresher air. He continued up to her stomach. When he got to her chest he stopped. Lifting each breast in turn, they were stiff and rubbery to the touch. Eric looked at them for a long time and then nodded to himself. He took his knife and cut out her left breast, placing the lump of flesh on the sheet next to her. He cut deeper into her chest until his knife touched the bones of her rib cage. Then he dug in with considerable strength and pulled her ribs apart. He fished out her heart. The effort left him panting for air and the heart squashed and broken. With delicate precision he placed her heart in the middle of her chest and then he reached over and picked up her left breast. He turned it over and placed the tortured flesh back into the receiving hole. Then he continued moving up her body.

At her neck he stopped again, inspecting the gash that lay jagged across her skin, like a second mouth forever set in a scream. He reached into the gash, pulling it further open, till the hole went all the way through her windpipe, he found her tongue and with some effort he managed to pull it out. He laid it down the outside of her throat. Then he continued, up to her face. He stopped at her eyes, using his knife he sliced the lids off. Then he stood up, towering over her, his feet planted next to her shoulders. Looking down at his work he smiled to see his vision made real. She was glorious.

Her heart was exposed so all could see the ugliness that lived there, her tongue, her lying deceitful tongue, exposed for all to hear that which she could no longer say. And her eyes finally opened for all time, so she could look up at the beauty of the man that had made her anew. Eric stayed like that for the longest time, revelling in the glory of his creation.

Light as a tom cat, he jumped off the bed, the carpet was warm on his bare feet. He turned like a dancer and tiptoed to the bathroom, naked, blood spattered, graceful as if he were swimming through the pudgy air. There he began to fill the bathtub with warm water. While the Tub was filling he found his overnight bag, unzipped it and started unpacking his sanitation kit placing each item neatly on the porcelain edge. Once the water reached the desired level he lowered himself into the tub. Taking pleasure as the heat seeped into his skin. Eric submerged his torso. He took the wash cloth, dipped it into the water. He wrung the hot water out over his chest and then he placed the steaming cloth over his face. Relaxation enveloped him. He felt warm inside and out, imagining what it must be like for a foetus cozied in the amniotic life giving fluid.

~~~

The afternoon sun poked lazy holes in the blanket of clouds that covered the sky. It had rained most of the morning and the world had that fresh washed smell. Puddles of dirty water lay all about and Eric absent mindedly splashed through them as he made his way home. Apart from being called into the Principal's office for being late again, the day carried the same dreariness of every other school day.

The Lectures failed to hold his interest. As usual he spent the day in the deep confines of his day dreams. During the first half of the day, under the influence of the drugs he smoked, his fantasies had no structure; he was an observer in his own imaginings and he let the stories play out of their own accord. Later, as the drugs wore off he found himself staring at Anna-Leigh. She was the prettiest girl in class and she held the attention of all the boys. For the last part of the school day he imagined that she was his captive. In his mind, he followed her home. He knew that both her parents worked during the day so he snuck up behind her as she opened the back door to her house. Once the door was open he clubbed her on the back of her head with a brick knocking her unconscious. Then dragged her limp body inside and locked the door behind him. Once inside he laid her on her back and tied her across the coffee table in the dining room. In his mind he waited for her to wake up, the idea of her confusion and panic when she woke was so visceral that he started to get an erection. In his mind he could see her struggle against the ropes in a futile effort to get free. Then as she began to comprehend what was happening she would lift her head and see him staring at her. In his fantasy, he was naked, holding his switchblade knife, a gift from his Uncle, he approached her. He slipped the point of his knife under her skirt, between her legs. His excitement growing, the knife gleamed in the diffuse light…

The last bell rang, and the class erupted into a confusion of movement. It took a few moments for Eric to impose his will over his thoughts. He packed his books neatly and the task helped to refocus his attention.

Half the class had already departed by the time Eric was able to stand. The herd of teenagers ignored their teacher who was reminding them about the weekend homework, as they all
~~~

clamoured to be free of the confining classroom. Anna-Leigh came up to Eric as he fastened the buckles on his book case. Arms folded across her chest, chin stuck out and a look of contempt on her face. She was backed up by her best friend, the insufferable, Jenna. "What's your problem!" she demanded. "Why do you keep staring at me?" She unfolded her arms; one hand went to her hip the other brought her pointed finger up into Eric's face. "You better keep your pervert eyes to yourself! Or I will cut off you tiny willie and make you eat it." Then she turned and wiped her ponytail into Eric's face. Jenna giggled and trailed after Anna-Leigh.

~~~

Eric felt cold. The wash cloth was stiff as he pulled it from his face. With every small movement of his body the icy water swirled around his naked flesh syphoning off more heat. His entire body was racked with shivers as his muscles tried to bring back heat to his body. He lifted himself out of the tub, his fingers numb. The white tiles were like sheets of ice on his bare feet. Eric stood motionless, hunched over against the cold for a long moment before he reached out and took the towel from its hook behind the door. He wrapped the towel around his shaking body in an attempt to fend off the cold.

Hunched over like a beggar he opened the door and moved into the bedroom. As he moved about the room he took special care to keep his eye averted from the bed. He was very much aware of what lay there, aware of what he had done, and the shame of it burned in his chest with the dull ache. Keeping his eyes down, he moved past the dresser, making sure that he did not catch a glimpse of his reflection. It was always like this. The Mouth that swallowed him and drove him to madness chewed him like cud and spat him up. It was always the same. The ecstasy of the dark left him a husk of self-loathing, and then there was the bitter after taste.

But this time was different. This time he had gone too far. This time the veil between fantasy and reality was penetrated. Eric dreaded this day for the longest time and his fear of it was like an old friend. He stole a look at the woman on the bed, a last attempt to undo what he knew he could not. While the rational part of his mind was busy working out how to clean up all the evidence of his deed, the rest of him was sick with fear and panic. He had an overwhelming sense of imminent danger and all he wanted to do was get out of the room and run off into the night but, his rational mind prevailed and kept him rooted in place.
~~~

Eric let the towel fall to the floor as he turned to face Anna-Leigh. He swallowed hard to keep from vomiting as looked at what he had done. He forced himself to keep looking while his mind worked out what to do next. He went back to the bathroom and retrieved the cleaning equipment from under the sink. For the next few hours he laboured till sweat poured from his skin as if his body was trying to clean itself from the inside. Working his way from the furthest corner of the bathroom to the front door of the hotel room, he made sure to remove all evidence that he had been there. When his task was complete he found himself standing at the front door, naked except for the pink latex cleaning gloves ill fitted to his hands. At his feet were two black refuse bags. One had all his bloody clothes; the other had the bloody sheets and pillow cases along with Anna-Leigh's clothes and all her possessions. Just a little off to his side was his overnight bag.

Still wearing the pink gloves he reached into the bag and pulled out his change of clothes. Once he was fully dressed he pulled his overnight bag onto his back, then he scanned the room to make sure he had not overlooked anything. Satisfied he hefted the refuse bags and opened the door.

The night air was warm and moist and the humidity made his skin feel immediately sticky. He locked the door and tossed the key back in through a half open window then he pushed the window frame back into place sealing the room like a mausoleum. Still wearing the pink gloves he carried the bags to his car. After depositing the bags in the trunk he climbed into the driver's seat, tossed his overnight bag onto the passenger side and started the engine. The radio squawked to life, and the monotonous beat of deep house music drowned out the sound of the pink latex as it squeaked against the steering wheel.

~~~

It was deep night and Eric could not sleep. In his mind he played back the scene from earlier that day with Anna-Leigh. This time when she brought her finger up to his face he grabbed it and twisted it sharply. Her eyes bulged in response to the pain as he forced her to her knees. Then he took out his penis, which in his fantasy was large and throbbing. He took hold of her neck and squeezed, lifting her onto the desk by her throat. His fantasy was cut short as light stole in through the door to his bedroom as it was pushed open. A shadow slipped inside like liquid darkness and closed the door behind it, shutting out the light.
~~~

Eric knew what was coming next, he could smell the alcohol fuelled breath of his Uncle as he crept forward in the dark. The shadow slipped under the blanket next to him and the mattress groaned under the added weight. Eric lay on his back and stiffened against his Uncle's first touch. He did not waste time, pushing his rough hands into Eric's pants. His whiskey-breathe harsh in Eric's ears, while whispering for him to be quiet. "It's OK… it's only me" he was saying. "Schhhhh".

The night sky was clear and the light from the street lamp was enough for Eric to make out solid shapes in the room. They appeared as silhouettes in the gloom. He focused on them as his Uncle turned him over and pulled down his pants. Eric concentrated on the shape of the bedpost in front of him. Tracing the line that formed between the gap in the wood. He focused on the shape to the exclusion of everything else.

The rectangle in the middle appeared like a dark bar across his vision, slowly the edges softened and the shape changed. In his mind the edges blurred until it looked like a mouth with dark cherry lips. It was moving toward him now, dark and wet. He felt the lips touch his forehead as sweat beaded there; the lips were cool and soft. They parted and he felt a slow sucking sensation in the centre of his forehead. The sucking increased until it started to hurt. The Mouth opened up, and swallowed his head. Pulling him forward it sucked him deeper and deeper into the wet dark. Eric gave in and plummeted forward. He felt like he was falling through a deep pit. The feeling of weightlessness made him feel like he was flying and the loss of control was so enjoyable he began to laugh. He fell faster and faster until all he felt was the profound joy of the fall.

~ The End ~

Vetalas Rising:

A Cautionary tale

By: Noel Daniels

Well, I suppose you want to know how I got here. The truth, believe it or not, is that I don't really know. Shit happens, what can I say. Fact of the matter is… here I am; tied to a fucking chair, chicken wire cutting into my burning wrists… food for the un-dead. Yes, yes yes, it's my own fault, I mean, OK I was tricked, but I let myself get tricked. I fell to temptation… man… even now I can't find the balls to be honest with myself. So let me try to be honest with you. It's all bullshit man. You know it and I know it. Venemeer certainly knows it. I let myself be deceived and soon he will devour me, feast on my sin. Christ… he'll become *Vetalas*; because of me. Fuck!

Forgive me…

Right. So. Here's my story, judge me if you want, fucked if I care. But be warned, there are no heroes here. Nah man, this ain't a tale of redemption or great adventure or any of that BS. No sir this is just the story of how I ended up here, nothing more. There's no escape for me son; no one is coming to rescue me. I'm doomed, lost, Venemeer's already won but maybe you'll learn something. Maybe my story will serve you in some way, but I leave all that to you. I will offer only the telling, disturbing as it is.

My story begins in 1968. The Vietnam War Crimes Working Group had just been formed in the wake of the *My Lai Massacre*, that shit was Fugazi man, a total clusterfuck. I was in the shit since 65', from day one, seen my fair share of blood and bush and let me tell ya, I don't blame those jarheads man, it was war for fuck sake, things get messy. Ain't never gonna be a clean war forget that with the fairytales man. So there I was, all of twenty one, at the ass end of a three year tour of duty, nothing but bush and bugs, romp and stomp and just hump'n for days. I was ready to go home, man, ready to crawl into a bottle for the rest of my days. But then I got the call to join the *Group*. I was more than happy to get away from the bullets. Perimeter watch in the endless goddamn rain was the worst. At the time I was just another grunt, I mean I was an officer but that don't mean shit in the Nam. Me? I joined up, volunteered straight out'a high school. Ready to do my part for god and country, a bona fide super lifer, so the only way I was going home was WIA, or a body bag.

I remember sitting there one night while mosquitos big as Huey's chomped down on my neck, toying with the idea of blowing off a toe or finger. The only thing that stopped me was the idea of getting a section 8, I mean, you gotta do it just right you know. So when I heard about the *Group* I applied for a transfer, I just got made a mustanger but I didn't want it. I didn't want to be responsible for no one but me. Anyway, it was a way off the frontline, nothing more. When word came down that I got approved I was jacked. Green lit for getting out of the shit. I mean I was still in country till the brass pulled the plug or we beat the gooks but I was out man, out of the bush I mean. No more point patrol in 100 degree heat. No more days of just marching through shit waiting for the pop of a SKS to tag me. And the gooks were only the half of it. I swear that jungle was alive, fucking two steppers, all over, spiders the size of cats, mud holes that would swallow a man, not to mention gook booby traps.

The *Group* was set up to investigate major incidents. What we ended up doing was covering Uncle Sam's ass everybody knows that. But there was the other side of it, the part no one likes to talk about, the part we all just wanna forget. L'me tell ya, some really weird shit goes down in war zones. We were all on edge all the time and that messes with your head. I mean, you musta heard of soldiers going all necro or whatever, but I ain't talking about the run of the mill PTSD shitstorm. You see, all that blood and death attracts the ghouls. I'm talking serious demonic shit from the depths of fucking hell brother. I'm talking about full blown cradle of Satan shit. Like this dubious fucker sitting over there in the dark right now, getting ready to drain me.

By the time I got my first solo assignment I was a *group* Vet. After 3 months with the group, I investigated everything from Giant Rock Ape sightings to Ghosts. But my first solo assignment was to investigate a report of some village girls that were found dead near *Buon Me Thuot*. The assignment was simple and straightforward on paper, but, man I was pissed man, they were found right in the thick of the shit right in the middle of the boonies. They dropped me right back in the shit I mean what's the point right, but the *Group* wanted to make sure we had nothing to do with it. The assignment to go in and make sure the cause of death was anything other than a bullet from a US issued weapon. It was a cover up, a forgone conclusion. I was under no illusion as to what my role was, just politics I guess. I was there to find the right kind of evidence. For my own part I just wanted to get the job done asap and bug out. In and out before Charlie pushed south again and that meant I was looking for anything that would confirm it was a gook skin job and thats it.

The Village was about 10 clicks North West of *Buon Me Thuot*, surrounded by some of the thickest bush in the Nam. I was there for months on scout petrol so I knew that stretch of bush well enough. I knew I'd be choper'd in to the closest LZ with a group of jolly greens fresh off the boat and then we'd hump in through the bush. Fresh meat you know. Charlie liked setting up camp in the trees and taking pot shots at the choppers, so we came in hot. The LZ was barely 150 feet, the pilot hovered for 30 seconds, just long enough for us to haul ass. Bushmaster Patrol poured out of the tree line as soon as the bird was clear. They were real operators I could see by the way they moved. The five man crew stood calmly in the sweltering heat, sharing knowing looks as they inspected the new recruits. They pegged me for a vet as soon we made eye contact. The Sergeant called for us to fall in and we did. The new citizens stumbling up behind, no one gave a shit. They were just fodder man. They had a VC tracker with them too and even he was eying the trees like they would come alive any second. As we marched I listened to the Gunny, a massive navy-blue motherfucker bring the new citizens up to speed. The bush ain't a joke son, and no one wanted to buy the farm on account of a cherry.

We got to the village just as my nerves were getting brittle. I can't tell you how much I hate the bush man. I swear those trees have eyes. It was quiet. The battalion was gathered at the mouth of the village like they were afraid to go in. Who ever heard of mother green getting chicken legged on account of some backwater gooks, something was up, I could just feel it. The thing that struck me was how quiet they were. No one jibed the cherries; they all just stared at us with hollow eyes. The Sergeant led us through the village, the silence more stifling than the humidity. Even the Gooks were quiet. The man in charge was sitting in the shade of the busted hut. All that was left was the mud wall. As we came up to him he stood and leaned back against the wall, he smiled at me. It was like something out of a John Wayne movie. "My, my, my… welcome to paradise boys", he said. His accent smooth as Virginia silk. The men called him Slenderman on account of being tall with lanky limbs that gave him a distinctly spider-like quality.

He inspected his replacement troops and waved 'em up. Then he focused on me. The first thing he wanted to know was what in the damn hell I was supposed to be doing in his bush. Nothing in his manner gave me the impression of being annoyed, more interested in what the *Group* was expecting by sending me out there. You see Slenderman was of the opinion that the only good gook, was a dead gook. Kill'em all and let God sort them out. Now, like I said before I was under no illusions as to what I was doing there, so I told him, "just here to cover Uncle Sam's ass. Gotta make sure the folks back in the world don't get the wrong idea of what we doing out here". "Heard that" he said. He was smiling the whole time. I mean what did he have to be so cheerful about.

Now, these girls were found 5 days before I got there, figured I could get a look at the bodies, check for bullet holes and what not and be on my way. Figured I could move out with the next inbound supply bird and write up my report on the way back to Base Camp. Tell ya the truth I wanted to get back to Karen, this Doughnut Dolly I met when I was in the DMZ. Let me tell ya… She had a great ass and titties to match, a man can't ask for much more than that, you know. She was a little older than me but that didn't matter much in the Nam. Turned out the bodies weren't in the village. No one in Bravo company was gonna haul them out of the bush, and the local gooks didn't wanna touch'em.

Slenderman suggested I get some chow and then talk to the old man that found the girls, after that I could decide if I wanted to see the bodies. Sounded good to me so I agreed. The food was as good as you're gonna get in the bush, hot and brown, lots of beans and weird ass meat. Never ask about the meat, brother, you don't wanna know. After I ate my fill I went to find Professor, the Lt said he was the only one that talked gook. I found him with the rest of the juicers, he was mighty pissed off when I told him what was up. I was cutting into his R and R so it was to be expected. But orders were orders, and you don't fuck with the chain of command.

Professor led me out of the village, it was pissing rain and the ground was all mud and rotting leaves. We must have walked for the better part of an hour before we came up to the little mud house. It looked like it was literally growing out of the mud. Outside standing in the rain was a man so old he could'a been standing there for all of time. He was a tiny little shit, the size of a kid, but his bald head and wispy silver beard gave him away as a Papa San. He was waving his skinny arms and shouting something in gook. Professor talked to the little fucker and he seemed to calm down. But he creep'd me out, man, the whole time they talked he stared at me. I told Professor, to tell him, to tell me, everything he could about how the girls were found. The old man talked and Professor translated but they were talking way too fast. He talked for a long time, of course I didn't understand a fucking word, but one thing he kept saying over and over was, "ma ca rong." I asked professor what it meant… Vampire… can you imagine that shit. A fucking gook Vampire man. Except it wasn't a gook, but we'll get to that later.

The girls were well known in the area, they were Boom Boom girls, according to the old man they were lured out of the village by the"ma ca rong" with promises of a better life. How he knew that was beyond me and the red flags went up immediately, but I ignored them cause all I wanted was out of the bush. The girls were dead so I couldn't exactly ask them. He told his story as if it was nothing strange. Apparently when he was a boy, the "ma ca rong" had already been active for years, a kind of bush boogeyman, a campfire scary story. But over the years they found bodies from time to time, torn up but no blood, that's how you know it's a "ma ca rong". It was clever too. The way the old man told it, it was like genius level smart. Listening to him, I realized that he had no fear of this thing. It seemed that he had some sort of weird boner for it. That alone got me thinking his story was BS. It turned out the old man was a "bac si phu thuy", a witchdoctor. That was why he lived so far outside the village. Or maybe he was just a sicko, maybe he killed them and was just trying to cover his tracks, anyway, that's what I figured at the start. The villagers shunned him of course, but they turned to him sometimes for protection against the supernatural. Apparently he made a deal with the "ma ca rong" on behalf of the village. They would make gifts of their dead to feed it and the demon would leave them alone. The killing of the village girls broke that deal. The more I listened to the story the more fascinated I got. The old man made friends with it, he was helping it, he was a fucking demon groupie. I mean I didn't believe a word of what he said but it was a great fucking story. I made up my mind before we left his hut. He killed the girls, I was sure of it.

For all I knew the old man was a VC Jack the ripper. One thing was for sure, this wasn't gonna be a quickie bush jump. Fuck the *Group* and fuck politics man, I had to get to the bottom of this. It was just too fucked up to let go. I asked the old man to tell me more about how the bodies were found. For the first time he spoke English. "Better you see", he said. "Tomorrow, better you see". So the next day we hiked deeper into the bush. And I mean deep bush. Charlie was on the move to the North of us, so we had to move fast. The guys were on edge, the old man was on edge, if Charlie decided to move south we'd be cut off for sure. Maybe we'd get zapped, maybe we'd end up in a POW camp. But fuck it I had to see the bodies for myself.

Until I saw the bodies, I was convinced there was a normal explanation. I made up my mind that this Papa San did it and all I had to do was find the evidence. But what I saw still gives me the heeby geebies, even after everything I've seen since, even after Rwanda.. but, we'll get to that soon enough. So these girls had been lying out in the jungle for 8 days in the humidity, in pissing down rain, exposed to jungle bugs and God knows what else. I was expecting, well I don't know what I was expecting. But fuck me brother what I found was creepy as balls.

It looked like they had been ripped to pieces; their arms and legs were hung up in the trees, their torsos laid out on the ground. Their heads were pinned to the trees, the eyes were gone. All their organs had been removed leaving the body cavity open like screaming mouths. But that wasn't the worst of it. The thing was… there was no blood. Not a fucking drop. No bugs, no decomposition, none of that shit. I've seen a lot of dead bodies in my time, but this was the first time I saw something like this. They were posed, the bodies were arranged that way to send some type of message. Of course I didn't know it at the time but this was the work of Venemeer and his message was for me.

Ok I know what you're thinking… and you're right, this is the part where I'm supposed to convince you that vampires are real. Well like I said, I'm not here to convince you of shit, so you can cram it up your ass. All I'm here to do is tell you a story. Hopefully I'll get to the end before I bite it. It just so happens that it has to do with vampires and it just so happens that vampires are real. But, you need to forget everything you think you know about these undead fuckers. Well not everything, they ain't dead, and they drink blood, that part is real. But forget the rest. They have no issues with sunlight. And forget crucifixes. They're not animals that snarl and screech, and they don't shape shift… They're beautiful, I mean truly beautiful. They move with all the grace of dancers. They're not faster or stronger than humans. But they are… well they're just more. And just so you know, I have no idea how to kill'em. Like I said this ain't a hero story. I don't know how many of them there are, or where they came from. Here's what I know for sure. There are two types. The Vetalas and the Alukah. But we'll come back to that later.

Ok boys and girls, strap in cause it's gonna get dicey. Again… you don't have to believe me but here it is. So when you die, your soul gets trapped in your body. There's no heaven or hell, well not in the way you think. If you lived a good life, you go into a kind of sleep, until the Judgment, then you get a new body and you get to live in heaven, dance under rainbows and fuck unicorns. But if you're a piece of shit, well then you get the fun part, you're awake the whole time, trapped in your body for all time, and make no mistake, you can feel everything. But that's not the worst of it, trust me. Here's the good news kids, you can make a deal with a demon. I have no idea how many different types of demons there are, all I know is what Venemeer told me, so I don't know much, and he lies so I can only tell you what I experienced first hand. Some demons bring you back, same like you were before, no powers. Some can make you stronger, faster, or prettier than before. Some bring you back as you are at the moment you make the deal, rotten or fresh. But the fine print is always the same. You will be a slave to the demon. That's the deal, take it or leave it.

Getting back to the Boom Boom girls. What I stumbled into was a Vetelas ritual; one of seven. The short version is that the Alukah can become Vetelas by performing the rituals of "Dei ad mortem Ponticus" . I'm sure you think you know where I'm going with this and maybe you do, but then again maybe you don't know shit. Or maybe I'm a section 8 and I'm in a little padded room talking to the fucking walls right now. One thing that was crystal clear at this point, was that this had nothing to do with mother green. The girls weren't killed by bullets. I decided I wanted to take a closer look at the bodies but of course no one wanted to give me a hand. The old man went mental when he realized what I was planning but I was determined and so I went to work cutting 'em down. They were still limp, no rigor mortis, and the flesh was still warm to the touch, as if they were killed only a couple of minutes earlier. By the time I was done it was well after noon and the humidity was just ridiculous. I was hungry so I joined the others where they set up camp a few meters away. That Papa San stared daggers into me man. He kept saying "mao pham… mao pham mao pham!" fucking annoying. Professor told me later it meant desecrator. At the time it just pissed me off, so I cracked him on the side of the head with a spoon. He was quiet after that, but it ruined my chow time, and the little gook just kept staring at me.

I inspected the bodies, looking for clues, trying to figure out what killed them. At the back of my mind I was starting to think it really was a vampire, but of course I just pushed that shit aside. It still sounds crazy to me now man. I mean for fuck sake, vampires, in the Nam, out in the fucking boonies. But I tell ya, the more I looked at those bodies the more it made sense.

I was lying on my back later that night, staring at the stars that peeked out in between the trees. The Nam was hard, gruesome and downright cruel, but every now and then it was beautiful. It was crazy man, I mean just a minute before I was trying to figure what happened to those girls, the image of their limbs hanging in the trees like strange fruit still fresh in my mind and now I was admiring the night sky. The bush was alive with night sounds, the chirping of the crickets and the chorus of the cicadas grew louder till it was deafening. It was like they were inside my head, and then it just stopped. It was like a pop to silence. As I sat up, everything went black, I couldn't see shit. It was so dark, like my eyes stopped working.

That's when I heard him. The air was humming, electric with static as he moved toward me in the dark. I knew it was him, I could feel it in my bones. A cold dread mixed with excitement. It was like my blood was on fire but it was a cold fire. He came through the trees, his movement jerky as if he was lit by a strobe light and he was all I could see. Now, I don't go in for men, got no issue if you do, but fuck he was… Well he was beautiful. It was like he was lit from the inside, you know what I mean? He was an exotic creature. It was like he stepped out of another world.

Captivated as I was, he scared the bejesus out of me. It was at that moment that I understood how he got the girls to follow him. I couldn't think of anything else, he was inside my head before I knew how to react. He took me over and I let him in. It was like a door opened in my soul and he walked in, like he owned the place. It was power, full on, pure power.

He came right up to me and took my hand. It was hot, I mean you would'a expected him to be cold but he wasn't, his skin was hot, like a fever. He told me his name and then he pulled me into the bush. Looking back at it now I couldn't tell you why I went with him. I knew what he was even if I tried to deny it. When you meet one, you know. Your whole body will scream it at you. Maybe if I was a stronger person I could'a resisted, but he wanted me for something and he had no intentions of letting me go once he got his hands on me. I wanted to go with him. I wanted to be him and in the back of my mind I knew that from the start.

I don't remember everything that happened next. It was like being fucked on acid, reefer and booze all at once. It was like the tail end of it you know, like it still feels good but your body is rejecting it. The world turned around me, I wanted to vomit, I felt wonderful and horrible at the same time. I had no control over anything and I was sure I was about to buy the farm. When it stopped he was gone and I was left with what I can only describe as a yearning. I came back to myself but I knew I was gone. There was no going back to the world after that. Even then I knew it was about wanting to become like him. I always wanted to be powerful, to feel like what I did in life was somehow worthwhile. But it was more than that. I wanted to be free of the weight of the world. I mean that's why I joined up. At least that's what I thought I wanted. Turns out I wanted power, pure raw undiluted power. I wasn't there for meaning, nah man, turns out I wanted to assert my will on other people. Turns out that was the reason I hated the Nam. All I did was follow orders; all I did was listen to lesser men. All I did was hump, day in and day out carrying the sins of politics. I was playing at war just like the rest of them. Only we had real guns. And now here I was, face to face with a Vampire, I wanted what he had, I wanted to be him.

I was missing for nearly 2 days. Slenderman was just about ready to report me MIA. I was near madness, certified man. Section 8. I had it in my head to gear up and go looking for him. But Slenderman put a pin in that shit real quick. On top of that, word came down from the *Group*, they wanted me back in the DMZ to report in. But I had other plans. The supply bird was inbound, 0800… but I had other plans.

In the Nam there was hundreds of ways to die when it wasn't your idea, but it was surprisingly difficult to fake it. My idea was simple: disappear into the boonies and get lost. Then when the company moved out I could start looking for him. Only problem was I came back with crazy written on my forehead. So the Lt put a guy on me. Rat was short, thin, but wiry. You know the type, looked like the wind could just blow him away but he was strong. I knew the minute I saw him there was no giving him the slip. He watched me closely for a couple of hours, but he was deep into his tour. Funny thing happens in the bush, when you first get there you can't sleep. Fear, bugs, adrenaline… it keeps you awake. But after a while, you get numb. By the time you got 2 or 3 months under your belt you could sleep anywhere, standing, sitting, fuck I saw a guy sleep on the march one time. So I watched him, watch me. We both listened to the sounds of the bush… buzz, buzz, slap and those god damned cicada's. Soon enough his head started dipping.

The idea was like an afterthought, it was already in motion before it was fully formed. I wish to god I could take it back. That was the moment I lost everything. In life there are certain lines and once you cross'em, ain't no way back. But it was done before I could even think it through. I waited till deep in the night, musta been 4 or 5am, I moved quietly, I took Rat's K-BAR from his holster, and drew it across his throat. To this day I can't believe how easy it was. He opened his eyes and I could see it on his face. Fear, confusion, anger. He bled out in less than a minute. He tried to scream off course but the slice I made was across his vocal chords and the more he struggled the faster he bled out. I took the rest of his gear and slung him over my shoulder. He was heavy, or maybe I was just weak from the knowledge that I done him wrong. Sometimes when I think about it I can still feel the heat of his blood as it poured on my back followed by the sticky coldness as it cooled.

I was declared section 8 of course and reported MIA… Dishonorable discharge in absentia. As far as Uncle Sam was concerned I never left the Nam. If they found me they'd have done me, they'd a strung me up in the trees for what I did to Rat they'da blamed the gooks. There's no greater crime than murdering your own. But I tell ya the torment that waited for me was punishment enough.

 Venemeer broke me, physically and mentally. He toyed with me for years and now... well we'll get to that soon enough. I don't deserve redemption, I deserve to die or worse. I can accept that… ain't no heroes here man. For what I've done, for what I've become… fuck!... All I wanna do is take this undead sack a shit with me. I mean why does he get a reward? Why does he get what he wants? Fuck fairness man, ain't about that. He deserves death more than I do. I should be the one to feast on him, I should be the devourer of his sin. I SHOULD BECOME VETALAS!

But life doesn't work that way boys and girls. Life is what it is and you have to make peace with what you are in the end.

So I carried Rat deep into the bush. I had no idea how to find Venemeer, but I knew where to start looking. Man I tell'ya the look on that Papa San's face when I kicked his door in. I threw Rat down in front of him. He made no sound, he knew what I wanted. "For the mac ca rong" I said. I left him there and made my way deeper into the Bush. I had it in my head that Venemeer would find me, that he wanted to find me. I thought that if he wanted to kill me then he would have done it already. I was right. But the fucker made me work for it. I musta walked around the bush for a week. Dodging the patrols was the easy part. I lived on what the bush provided... you guessed it, bugs, grubs and roots. I had plenty of water but it wasn't fun. As the days drew on, I was sure they'd catch me, but I pushed on desperate to find Venemeer. In the end it was a snake that got me.

I never felt it bite me, it was only when my vision got blurry and my legs started getting numb that I realized something was wrong. At first I thought it was Venemeer, I thought finally he's come for me. I sat up against a tree and waited. I was excited if you can believe that, but as the time passed and my thoughts got slower, and my breathing heavier it became clear to me that I made a mistake. It was the end. Fuck was I pissed. I died. And there's nothing glorious about it, nothing romantic. Like I said, if you're a piece of shit you get the fun part. I couldn't move, I couldn't open my eyes. At first I thought I was just paralyzed or maybe I was hoping. But that wasn't it. The thing about death is that once you bite it, you know. There ain't no white light and no tunnels. You just know. One minute you're alive and the next you're not. It was the cold that fucked with me the most. I always hated being cold. For me it was the coldness of being dead that was the worst. As I laid there I kept thinking about Rat.

It didn't take long for the ants to find me and they went right to work. I could feel them crawling all over me, itchy little fuckers. Soon enough I felt the first bite, then another, then another and another. They were all over me. My face and my hands got the worst of it. They crawled inside my nose, under my eyelids, into my ears. I screamed in my head. It was all I could do. I could hear the mosquitos and the flies buzzing round my head. I knew what came next, I mean what comes after the ants and the flies. I knew I was worm food. There was no hope, none. You don't know madness till you die, that I can tell ya. But true madness is when you accept what is happening.

I stayed like that for days, I could smell my flesh as it rotted. I was in a permanent state of panic, suspended in disbelief. All I kept thinking was I'm not dead, I can't be... but I knew I was, and when it happens to you, you'll know too. I couldn't figure it out and I refused to give in to the truth. I mean it was obvious but my mind wouldn't let me accept it. I was rotting and I was being eaten by the bush. Then came the rodents. By the end of the second night they gnawed into my stomach, I mean I could feel them crawling around inside of me man. The pain was constant, but the funny thing is I kinda got used to that. It was the feeling of them crawling inside me that fucked me up, that, and the fucking cold. That's when he came to me. At the very outer edge of madness and by the time he came I was ready to agree to anything just to stop the fucking rats. He told me what was happening to me, and he made me an offer.

I told him where to get off. I mean I was in pain and scared out of my mind. And of course part of me just simply didn't believe what was happening. I don't know how long I was rotting, but once Venemeer got there he never stopped talking. He just wouldn't shut up. He went on and on about fuck knows what. To be honest I was only half listing, but the gist of it was this:

He was Alukah, a Vampire. He was born a man and turned when he was in his late 30s at a time when that would have made him an elder. As Alukah he was bound to his maker. He was a slave. He could be freed in two ways; His maker could kill him or he could kill his maker, but, Venemeer had found a third option… Vetalas. He offered me a deal, the same deal he was once given. He would turn me, resurrect me, and in return I would be Alukah and he would help me to become Vetalas, as he once helped his maker to Rise. After he became Vetelas he would share the secret of "Dei ad mortem Ponticus" with me, and I too would Rise.

That was the deal, that was the line of BS he fed me and I ate it up. He didn't need to convince me of shit. I wanted to be like him, but I resisted. I didn't like the part about being a slave. That's the part that kept me from agreeing right off the bat. So he kept talking as the Rats kept running through me.

Eventually I was found by Bushmaster patrol, musta been weeks, maybe months later. The same guys that met us at the LZ, I heard the squad talking and I recognized their voices. The bush bugs had taken my eyes, but for some reason I could still hear perfectly. By then I had accepted everything Venemeer told me as truth, but when I heard the patrol decide to leave my body in the boonies, that's when it hit me. It was the final fuck you, I was done man. They just left me there. Worst still, they said I deserved it and maybe I did, but fuck them you know.

I laid there for a long time after that. I came to know later that he was watching me the whole time. Waiting for the right moment. When Venemeer came back I was so fucking relieved that I accepted his offer. I mean I was out of my mind by then, I would'a done anything just to move, to feel something other than the pain and that god awful loneliness, that feeling of being abandoned. He brought me back to life, well, he made me undead. It hurt like a mother fucker. That must be what napalm feels like, like liquid fire all over. My flesh grew back on my bones. It felt like I was burning for days but when it stopped I felt glorious. I had never felt so good. Everything was crisp; my senses were awake for the first time. It was like going from black and white to color TV.

But the feeling was short-lived. When Venemeer said I would be his slave I didn't really understand he would be in complete control. Even my thoughts were his to command. From that moment on, I have been a prisoner in my body. And of course he lied to me. He was never gonna help me to Rise. He had other plans for me. Let me tell ya, this sadistic fucker, rapped my mind more than anything else. The things he made me do over the years twisted me. I became his toy, his plaything and he enjoyed tormenting me.

It's been nearly 32 years since that day. The turn of the century is looming and there is a distinctly apocalyptic feeling in the air. All this time I thought he just likes being cruel, you know just for the sake of it. I thought I was just entertainment, something to keep him amused. But, again I was wrong. He's been preparing for what comes next. You see, I'm the last one. He's been preparing me for the ritual. Fattening me up, like a lamb to slaughter. And I am fat with sin, soon he will feast on me.

By now I'm sure you're wondering what the Vetalas rituals are. Well the short version is that's how the Alukah Rises to become a more powerful Demon, a true Vampire. The word Alukah means leech, well loosely translated any way. You see when I became Alukah to Venemeer he started feeding off me. Not directly you understand. But any sustenance I get from the blood I drink is his to share, and he can take as much as he wants. So in a way he's the leech. If he wanted to he could cypher all my energy, killing me, but then he would have to make a new deal with another gullible asshole. I have to drink enough blood for both of us. But it's more than that, he feeds off my sin. So the more depraved shit I pull the stronger he gets and the stronger his hold over me. Its all kinds of fucked up man. He can control me, but if I do fucked up shit on my own its better for him. The Alukah can only make one slave at a time, if his maker allows it. But if you become a Vetelas, you can make as many as you want and the only way to Rise is to complete the seven Rituals. The Alukah has to devour the seven deadly sins as they manifest in blood. I know it sounds like BS. But I figure you got this far, you might want to hear the rest.

I'm sure you musta hear about the seven deadly sins. What you might not have heard about is this monk from Greece. Evagarius Ponitcus. He's the one that came up with this whole seven deadly sins thing. So according to Ponticus, these sins are a straight up ticket to hell. But here's the thing, the truth of history is in the details. All sin is manifest in the blood. If one of the seven deadly sins takes over your core being you become a living embodiment of that sin and an Alukah can consume you as sin. If they consume all seven sins in the right order they can Rise. The first Vetalas, the one Venemeer calls the First to Rise, wrote down how to do this in his manuscript, *Dei ad mortem Ponticus,* which loosely translated means, Death of the God of Ponticus.

Ok so let me break this down for you, it all starts with the Ritual of Gluttony *Ingeniosa gula rituali.* When Venemeer first became Alukah, he was like a mad animal. Insatiable. He was turned when he was in his late 30s. At the time he was considered well past his prime. He was born in the Netherlands at the end of the 13th century. He was some kinda Dutch noble, a Frissie something or other, fuck I can't remember all this shit, but he lost all his family wealth when they were conquered. Every now and then he'd get juiced up and start crying about it. Then he'd get angry and of course take it out on me. His maker was older, much older. From what I understand, an Alukah came over with the Vikings in the 10th century and set up shop in the Northern part of the Netherlands. He had an appetite for blood that could not be satisfied. He turned Venemeer so he could get more blood. That was it, he was just a gluttonous piggy kinda guy.

Together they drained entire villages. His maker could never get enough and so to survive Venemeer had to feed constantly. It drove him mad I think. It got to the point that they were hunted by the militia. It musta been real dicey, I mean it was the dark ages and the whole of Europe was obsessed with witch hunts and all that inquisition shit, but his maker was out of control. One thing I gotta say about Venemeer, his will to survive is unfathomable. It was clear that they had to slow down or they'd be caught. So he killed his Maker, somehow his will to survive proved stronger than the compulsion of his master and he drained him. I don't know the details of that story, and to tell you the truth I don't really want to know.

His maker was gluttony incarnate, so when he drank his blood he drank his sins. He drank hundreds of years of gluttonous depravity and stumbled into the first Ritual quite by accident. I can only imagine what that felt like, fuck if I could drain him I would, but his will I far greater than mine.

Free to do what he pleased for the first time in years, he traveled the world, looking for meaning in the dark places. His family was gone; everyone he ever knew was gone. He was alone in the world. But don't feel bad for him, at the end of the day, he chose to become a demon. And make no mistake, he loves what he is. He loves what he can do. After years of aimless drifting he found himself in Germany. There he came across a manuscript, written by the First to Rise. The first of the Vetalas, it became his obsession. And he began to plan out his own Rise. The manuscript is like a text book for ghoulish shit. It's a how to guide for spitting in the face of God. He still has it of course. He keeps it in a leather bound satchel and carries it everywhere. If I could'a got my hands on it then maybe I would be the one to rise.

Next came *ibidinis Omnis Fornicationis Rituali, the Ritual of lust and fornication.* Yep, you guessed it, the Boom Boom Girls back in the Nam. So, the soul of the victim must be befouled by one of the deadly sins. In this case lust. Once the sin causes enough damage so the victim believes they are enjoying themselves then they become the sin. It manifests in their blood. Every time those girls got fucked the sin of lust was acted out on them. It's the funniest thing in the world. No matter the type of abuse, if it goes on long enough the victim starts to think they deserve it, once they start to believe that then they start to enjoy it on some level. Psychologically, it's a coping mechanism, well that's what the headshrinkers say, but what do they know? It's the sin, manifesting in the blood. That's what Ponticus figured out, that's why he called them the seven deadly sins, I mean it happens with all sin but these ones are special.

When he drained the girls, he drank more than their blood. He drank the sins of all the men that abused them. He drank all that lust and it changed him just like the first Ritual did. He was now both gluttonous and lustful and I tell ya, that combination didn't work out well for me.

What I found out later is that he posed the bodies for me. He'd been watching me since I landed in the Nam. And he set me up good and proper. Just to let you know, the way they found the bodies had shit all to do with nothing, it was just his trick to get me interested. And yeah, it got me interested. It got me hooked.

After that came *Rituale avaritia, the Ritual of Greed.*

After the US pulled out of Vietnam we went to Australia. We rented a place in Cabramatta. The outside didn't look like much but we lived like kings. It was in the heart of the immigrant sector. A lot of the time it felt like the Nam was hell and we moved to the land down under where we were upgraded in status. It was a place of violence and depravity. It was like we picked up the worst parts of the Nam and polished it. Venemeer fucked everything he didn't kill, and most of the time that was me. But he also had another play thing. Her name was Tien. She was beautiful, dangerous and completely out of her mind. As I understand it, Venemeer knew her mother from the Nam and he smuggled her into Australia when she was maybe 9. If only her mother knew what he was planning.

He spoiled her in the light, she had the best of everything. But at night, in the dark, well let's just say what he did to her was unforgivable. The contrast between the day and the night is what drove her mad. To be honest I was more terrified of her than of Venemeer. I became like a ghost living between them. Sometimes, when she was still little she'd come to sleep by me, after he had his way with her. At first she'd cry herself to sleep, but that didn't last long. Thinking back on it now, what he was doing was so obvious it was cruel, but fuck it was brilliant in its depravity. First he would do something unspeakable, then he'd buy her something she wanted. He was programming her greed. He was making her associate stuff with love. He made a hole in the middle of her soul, and then he showed her how to fill it with things. Only the hole was too big so there could never be enough things to fill it. That's how greed works. The only thing that was ever going to fill that hole was love, and where in the fuck was she supposed to find that.

She was the envy of the neighborhood. She was what he made her. By the time she was 17 she ran the drug scene across the Auzy underworld. I mean she was ruthless. She fucked her way to into the bed of the leader of the 5T, but she was Venemeer's girl. He raised her to be a sacrifice. He gave her all the trappings of wealth, but he fucked her mind. He turned her into a Greed monster. It's like this, with Tien, if she wanted a slice of chocolate cake, she'd take the whole cake, eat her fill and bin the rest so no one else could get a slice. He mentored her depravity and then he drained her. It was sad, and it was the meanest thing he ever did. But the thing that made it so vile is how thought out it was. Every action he took against that girl was designed with one end in mind. At the end of the day you gotta give it to him man. He planned it all to the last detail. He set us up like dominoes. He took every advantage he could. Like a game of chess. Fucking pawn sacrifice man.

Then came *Rituale Romanum superbiae, the Ritual of Pride*. After he killed Tien, Venemeer was out of control and he knew it. I think he loved her in his own way. I mean he killed her without hesitation, but he loved her too. He raised her like she was a ripe apple, just a thing to consume, but I think it got to him. Maybe I'm just reading what I want into it. So maybe I can believe he's less of a monster. At the end of the day she's gone. But he was different after that. Maybe he just missed having her around to torment. All I know is that he changed after that.

I think he needed to put all the sins he had devoured into order so he left me in Australia. From what I pieced together he went to France. I don't know what he did there, He never told me and I never asked.

It was the best time of my life. I was left to my own devices. I mean I wasn't free, but that was the closest I ever got. You have to understand, that was the first time I was able to do what I wanted. I went to the Nam straight out of my parents' house. So this was the first time in my life where there was no one to tell me what to do and I gotta admit I went balls out crazy.

After I left Australia, I went to New York. I always wanted to go there and it was everything I could have asked for. Ah man, it really was the big apple, the night life, the girls, the drugs. I mean it was New York man. I used my connections with 5T and started dealing. It was the end of the 80's coke was out and H was in. I became an underground legend. I embraced the night. It really was the best time of my life. I even met a girl and fell madly in love. Her name was Jerry. I don't think she knew what I was but that didn't matter. She was easy to be with. OK she was a junky, and maybe she was so far gone she couldn't tell her ass from her elbow, but I loved her. Everything was great until I killed her. I can't say it was an accident, that implies it wasn't my fault. We used to play this game. She'd get high as fuck and I would feed on her. There ain't no greater high than that man. I'd take her just to the point of death and then one night I went too far. I kept the body, cause I knew she was still in there, and I talked to her so she wouldn't feel too lonely. I bleached her body so the worms couldn't get her, but I couldn't stop the rot. I took care of her. That's all you need to know about that.

After some years Venemeer sent me a letter, telling me to join him in Rwanda. I mean of all the back water shitholes in the world, fucking Rwanda. I buried what was left of Jerry, by then she was just bones so at least there's that. I did right by her in the end.

Anyway I went to find Venemeer. As soon as I saw him I knew that he had devoured the sins of some poor bastard. Like with all the rituals before, it took him over. It became part of him. I tell ya man, if I thought he was dick before, now he was a smug dick. Fuck my life right. Turns out he found some third rate former noble that was all pride and no substance. I never got all the details but it seems pretty straightforward to me. I mean think about it, all those old wealthy families have the same malfunction. They think they're better than the rest of us on account of being born. Fuck em, fuck em all. That's what pride is and that's what pride gets you. There's this great line from the bible, not that I'm into that kinda thing but, it goes like this… First cometh pride then cometh the fall.

Old Venemeer was getting close and we both knew, I couldn't help feeling admiration for what he had accomplished so far. I mean don't get me wrong, I still hate the fucker. But you gotta give him an A for effort. Next came *Rituale Romanum irae, the Ritual of Wrath* and Rwanda. There ain't never been anything worse than Rwanda man.

What were we doing in Rwanda? We were getting ready to feast. Looking back on it now it seems kinda fitting, I was having the greatest time of my life till I fucked up with Jerry and know I was getting my punishment. A one way ticket back to hell. I got there on Valentine's Day in 94 and the tension was like a second skin. It was like a blanket of fear and desperation. Everyone was on edge. Even on the worst day in the Nam shit never felt that bad. The whole place was ready to pop off. And when it did it was hell on earth… It was literally the worst thing I ever seen people do to each other. Let me tell ya, there ain't no greater hell than what man does to man, brother. It ain't the ghouls you gotta be scared of.

As soon as the Hutus started the attacks, we started feeding. Fuck, I mean nothing I can say can describe it. It was a total free for all, a cluster fuck of the most epic proportions. 8 days of complete depravity. Even now it makes me gag thinking about it. That was the worst 8 days of my life. Even worse than the days I spent rotting before he turned me, worse than watching Jerry rot away. I was filled with hate and anger, and the more blood I drank the more I hated. Fuck man, I can still taste it. Venemeer was in high spirits, he enjoyed it I think, me ? I just wanted it to end. I had my fill by the end of the first day, but Venemeer pushed me on till the end. Part of me thinks he had something to do with setting up the entire genocide, maybe I just don't want to believe that kind of evil lives in the hearts of men. This ritual was different from the others. There wasn't one point of sin like the others, it was just the compounded sins of a nation at war with itself. We fed and fed until all we were was wrath.

After Rwanda I was so depressed. All I wanted was to crawl into the fucking dirt and die. Venemeer was consumed with his own struggle, so he left me alone again… for a time. I mean he's the worst kinda fucked up I ever met and he needed a time out after that shit.

I lived like a beggar, nothing mattered to me, nothing and no one. I just walked for days on end, till I couldn't take the hunger and then I'd feed on whatever I could find. It didn't matter man, I fed on anything that had blood. I had this single thought in my head. I wanted to die. But I didn't know how to end it. So I just kept walking.

It wasn't long after that I met Jacob and by the end of that friendship I had handed Venemeer *Rituale quod acedia, the Ritual of Sloth.* Somehow I worked my way up to Lagos. I found Jacob living in the heart of the city. He wasn't poor by any means, he just didn't give a shit. He had no interest in anything. We became friends but even that was lazy. I mean we just kinda grifted together. I didn't put in an effort and I know he didn't. It was a friendship by non-consent. I don't even remember exactly how we met. He was just there one day. But we did everything together. Looking back at it now, he was sloth, like the embodiment of sloth. While I was in New York I read everything I could on the Seven Deadly sins. How I didn't see it coming I don't know, but it seems obvious now. I didn't care enough I think. But I knew he was sloth. I remember thinking one day he'd be the perfect vessel for Venemeer.

And then one day I found him, dead, drained. I was still deep in my own depression. But that brought me back. Venemeer killed him of course and in the same way he killed those village girls back in 68. The scene was staged for me. It was his design. I was out all morning, dumpster diving. I was looking for shit to sell you know whatever I could get my hands on. Glass was the big thing, finding glass was like finding gold. And I found a shit ton. I never thought through why there was so much in one place but I took it all down to the local dump. I got paid, got some beers and went back to the little tin shack to find Jacob.

Venemeer was there to greet me. To gloat over his kill. I could see it in him. But he fought it down. Sloth is the most difficult of all the Rituals. I mean think about. All the other rituals affected him, he became the sin. So the Sloth he consumed made him stop caring. The thing about Sloth is that it makes you lazy to the point where you don't want to try. But Venemeer was determined if he was anything and he was soon on to the next part of his plan. *Rituale Romanum inanis glorie, the Ritual of Vainglory.*

Seeing Jacob's body was like being dunked in cold water. It was like waking from a deep sleep. All the pieces fell into place. All this time Venemeer was preparing me to be the last one. This was his end game. I was his end game. Just like Tien he's been preparing me to be harvested. It's been a few years since Jacob. I knew this day was coming, fuck man… why am I such a coward? I mean I could have spent the last few years getting ready to fight, or enjoying the fuck out of life while I could. But no, I been hiding in bum fuck Nebraska hoping he wouldnt find me knowing he never lost me. He tied me to this chair, and he's been sitting in the corner wrestling with himself. I think we've been here for some days already, but he still hasn't moved. It's dark outside again and I think it might have rained, I can smell the earthy sand all through the cave.

Just so we are clear, so you understand. I am envy incarnate. All this time I wanted to be Venemeer. All this time I've been in awe of his power, his singular focus. Just like all the others I have been envied. And just like the others I am guilty of envy. That is my sin. Well that's the big one.

In high school I was what you might call a jock. I was popular. I was who the girls wanted and what the boys wanted to be. I made good grades, I could'a gone to College. I should'a gone to College. But, I went to Nam. I was envied in my squad, even when I joined the *group* I was envied by everyone I came across.I mean it all came easy to me. And the rest of the guys didn't get me. But they hated me, for being privileged enough that I chose to be in the Nam. And I don't blame them, but let me tell ya, they can have my life. I fucked up man. I mean I fucked up on every single thing in my life.

So there you have it boys and girls. There ain't no escape for me, I am his escape. He played me from day one. All this time he's been fattening me up. Feeding my envy. To tell you the truth, I am all the sins… Maybe that's why he kept me for the end. I am a glutton, for punishment and I cannot be satisfied. I am lustful, always have been, and just like the boom boom girls somewhere along the way I convinced myself I like being fucked. I am greed, I want everything, my desires far outreach my abilities, the more I get the more I want. I am proud, of what I can't tell you, I didn't achieve much in my life but in my mind I am the best at everything. I am wrath, I would destroy the world if I could, my anger boils in the heart of me like molten stones. I am sloth, I mean fuck, it's not like I ever really tried to be anything, I am a passenger in my own downward spiral. But more than anything I am envy. Every part of me, all my actions and my apathy all drips with envy. I envy this thing. This demon. I want to be it. I exalt it. I'm just like that old Papa San, I'm a Fucking demon groupie. I mean it never came into my mind to actually try and kill him, yes I thought about it but I just haven't got the balls to do it to really do it I mean. As much as I hate this undead piece of shit, he's the best. And that's the heart of it, he's better than me, that's what pisses me off.

It's like being in love, you know what I mean. He's ruined me, the last 30 years of my life has been a living hell. Literally. I mean how fucked up am I. In my mind, my sins are his. And when he's done with me, he will be Vetalas. So in a way I will be too. I could never pull it off anyway. But I wish I could. I wish I was like him. I wish I could kill him. I wish I could take his place. But mostly I wish I never met him. Then I could go about my mediocre life. Maybe I'd be an alcoholic, maybe I'd be a person of some substance who knows. But he came into my life and set the bar too high. I can't compete with that. At the end of the day I was a completely useless person. So what made you think I was going to be anything other than a useless Vampire. Like I said. There are no heroes here. This is not a story of redemption. He's already won man.

Ah… he stirs. He's moving in the dark. He's ready, looks like our time is up. He comes to claim me.

28

Hope is a four letter word

A Short story by: Noel Daniels

The Midday sun sat high in the sky like the king of all creation. Beating wave after wave of punishing heat into what remained of the house Jericho was using as a hide out for the day. It must've been something special before the wars. High ceilings, hard wood floors and the type after arched windows that let in just right amount of natural light. The last week or so had seen perfect weather, no rain and just the right amount of sun so that the night skies were clear and the moon and stars were visible. But it was still sweltering in the early hours of the morning when he stole into the house. It was the biggest house he had ever squattered in, and that made it dangerous by default. When he arrived early that morning he thought caution be damned. There was a good chance a house that big would still have a decent bed somewhere in one of those rooms and maybe a bed sheet that was passable.

He was on the second floor, another mistake. He was breaking all his rules just for some semblance of normality. If they came for him now he had nowhere to run. But his suspicions had provided a bounty of creature comforts. The room he was in must have belonged to a teenager. The walls were plastered with faded posters of boys. Teen heartthrobs with pouty rose colored lips, sporting the fashions of their day. Bright colored hair doos faded now from exposure to the elements, looking even more ridiculous after so much passage of time not to mention the impracticality. Jericho wondered what was the point as he made his way around the room. The bed was huge taking up half the room, four postered with a tattered princess net. The sheets were dusty but gloriously soft after so many days of roughing it in whatever hole he could find.

Jericho laid cozy under the blanket, it was stiflingly hot, but he didn't care. It had been so long since he felt any kind of comfort that the sweat stain forming under his body bothered him very little. The house also still had running water another bonus in the bounty provided by the house, so he knew he could chance the loss of hydration. Throughout the day he kept drifting in and out of sleep while fever dreams wracked his mind. Some were happy dreams, strange and colorful, like being inside a spinning rainbow as images from his early childhood mixed with fantasies of what he wanted his life to be. Others were pure nightmare, or maybe they could be called daymare, filled with running and blood, and terror. By the time the sun started setting, the bad dreams started mixing with the good, like rotten fruit spoiling the bunch and when he opened his eyes, there were no more good thoughts in his head. Only the dread terror, of them.

There was a rustling in the room, Jericho lay still under the blanket, hardly daring to breathe. He listened intently, trying to make out the tell tail sound of metal, sliding over metal. With his heart thudding in his ears, he peeked his head out of the blanket. The sound was now clearer. Something was sniffing at the base of the bed. His initial fear of them subsided and was replaced by a more manageable fear as he started to wonder what kind of animal was sniffing around the bed. The fact that it was looking for him wasn't obvious; he might be squatting in its bed for all he knew. But was it something with claws and fangs? Or was it one of the mutated mutts, gangly creatures that survivors of the war referred to as howlers. Whatever it was he knew that if he could manage to kill it before it killed him he was having fresh meat for a change.

The creature popped up on the bed, and by the weight of it he knew he had the advantage of strength, whatever it was, it was small enough to manage in a fight. Either way he had to be both patient and agile. He waited for the creature to move up over his body, from the way it sniffed he thought he had it pegged for a howler which meant he had to kill it before it knew what was happening. Howlers… well they howl, when they get startled or when they get hurt, and that would bring… them. There was just enough daylight left that if one of them was near enough they could still get him. It was a hard choice. If he waited too long he risked losing his dinner, so far the creature was not aware of his presence but that could change at any moment. If he messed up the timing the howler would alert them and they would come to eradicate all life they found. He decided to wager an empty stomach over the possibility of startling a howler. His patience was soon rewarded. The Howler wasn't looking for him, it was looking for a place to bed down for the night, maybe he was a squatter after all but something about the way it moved made him think this was both of their first time in this place. Jericho felt the creature turning its body round and round on a spot of the bed a few inches from his chest. He listened as the creature's breathing became regular and deep. Once he was confident it was asleep, he snuck his hand to the Buck Knife on his utility belt and softly unclipped it from the holster. Moving in dead silence he came up out of the bed sheet moving with aching slowness so that he did not cause the bed to creek.

It was a howler, one of the leathery ones. It looked like a skinless dog but it only had two legs both curled up so that the legs covered the tiny beak shaped snout. Still moving with excruciating slowness Jericho got into position. Once he was ready to strike he moved like lightning. He grabbed the creature by the snout and drew the sharp edge of his knife across the creature's neck, nearly decapitating it. The blood spurt hitting the wall and covering some teenage boy's face with hot gore was the only sound. Jericho smiled to himself, everything went perfectly to plan. He cleaned the blood off his knife using the bed sheet and put it back in the sheath on the utility belt. Then he reached down and pulled a smaller skinning knife from the ankle holster then he started gutting and skinning the gangly creature. There wasn't much meat to be had but it was better than the unknown contents of the labless tins in his backpack. You never knew what you were having for dinner when it came to tins from the old world, sometimes you lucked out with some fruits in syrup but most of the time it was beans or mushroom soup. If you were unlucky you got food poisoning, lots of fun in the daytime when all you want to do is be quiet while you are hiding from them. And if you were really unlucky you got death. Vomity, diarrhearry, stomach achey death

It tasted gamy, that was to be expected, but Jericho's joy at having fresh meat was short lived after the first bite. The meat was bitter and he ate as much as he could stomach out of necessity. Out in the wilds, on the road food is food and you don't waste meat no matter how bad it tasted. Once he had his fill he wrapped the rest up in a piece of cloth he cut from the bed sheet, threw the innards and skin on the fire and added more wood. Watching the flames was hypnotic, but he had to resist the urge to add more wood. Once the fire started dying, that was the signal that he needed to move on to the next task while the night was still young.

He moved through the house trying to make out the shapes of anything useful in the dark. The stars were bright in the sky so that helped but it was still slow going. Jericho persisted because he knew there would be something worth his time in a house that big. Something to trade, maybe some tinned food that raiders in the past had missed, maybe a good knife, some sporting gear that could be deployed as protective armor, something. After a good hour of searching he hit the jackpot. On the first floor, in what could have been a den or a private office he came across a broken bookcase. Behind it was a panic room. The owner had tried to hide from them, but they managed to get in, they always get in. The panic room door was torn open by something incredibly powerful. The entryway was streaked with blood, it was old and dusty, the lonely hand with the black blood trail that lay a few feet inside was somewhere between skeleton and mummified, the question of where the rest of the body was made for more nightmare fuel. Inside was a weapons cache. Riffles, Handguns, Semi automatic machine guns, and enough ammunition to supply a small army. Jericho wasted no time, he went straight for the handguns and outfitted himself like the heroes in the action movies he loved as a young man. He was kind of upset that he couldn't take the lot, but he was on foot, so he had to be practical.

In the end he settled on four handguns that all used the same ammunition and a snub nosed shotgun. The owner of the house must have been a gun nut, because Jericho also found holsters for all the weapons including ammunition pouches. The Glock 17 went on his belt, right side. The Sig Sauer went on a shoulder strap under his left armpit. A second Sig Sauer compact went in a holster on his right thigh and the Beretta went into the backpack's concealed carry space. The best part for Jericho was when he strapped the Shotgun to his back on a concealed leather chord. "Badass!" he thought. It was a TSD 870 and Jericho knew he was being a bit of an idiot for getting all giddy about this find. He felt ridiculous but at the same time he felt powerful. He transferred all his gear to the new backpack he found, but there was still a ton of hardware left over. One thing Jericho had learned in this world, was never leave a treasure you can't carry for someone else to find. This world was a selfish one and you had to be selfish to survive. His first thought was to bury it, but the time it would take to dig a whole big enough and deep enough to to cover an arsenal that size was time he didn't have. But burying the weapons still left open the possibility that someone could find them. Then he saw it. The Steal Crate was about two meters across with the word "AMMONIUM NITRATE" stenciled across it in bold black letters and Albemarle Corporation below that. The question of what it was doing there didn't cross his mind. All his thoughts were bent on how he could use it to destroy what he couldn't carry. Before his plan was fully formed he was already searching for some military grade C4. There had to be some… there just had to be.

It didn't take long for him to find what he was look8ng for. He had to be precise or the explosion would draw the attention of every kind of nasty in the visual blast radius, and a house that big would burn for hours after. The worst case scenario would be to attract one of the hunter tribe patrols. Humans were the most dangerous creatures on the road, you never knew what level of desperate they were. Best thing to do would be to booby trap the place somehow. The hope being that he would be long gone by the time something set it off. But that was unreliable, what if it failed. It was just too much gear to leave for anyone to find. This was the kind of find that could turn the tide in the tribe wars and if that lunatic Jackal got hold of it… well that would be a disaster to put it mildly. Jericho made up his mind years ago to go alone into the wilds and that alone made him a target but the thought of Jackal's hunter tribe being armed to the teeth with this level of hardware was too much. He had to do something.

In the end he decided on a delayed detonation. It was the kind of job he was good at, he had spent years salvaging electronics from the ruined homes of the old world for just this kind of job and he was good at it. As long as he found good wiring in the walls he could make it work. He was breaking yet another one of his rules. He didn't like taking chances, but what else could he do? For the next hour or so he dug into the walls and got the wires he needed. In the master bedroom he found a clock radio that was perfect for the timer. Next he wired up the place and arranged the ammonium nitrate in a way that would cause the house to fall in on itself to limit the time the house would burn, at least that was the plan. He also had to give himself enough time to put some distance between himself and the house. All this work took him the better part of the night but it was necessary. As he figured it, he would still have enough time to find a new place to bed down for the next day.

Jericho was on the hike pushing hard into the night,when he heard the explosion and as soon as he did he knew he fucked up. It was much louder than he anticipated and the plume of smoke and fire reached high into the sky. But that was only part of it, it was too soon. He miscalculated something, it should have been at least another hour before he heard anything other than the night bugs. Instinct took hold of him like the hand of God. He was running flat out before he even fully registered the explosion, his mind racing faster than his feet. On and on he went till his fingers felt numb, instinct took over, his eyes automatically scanned the dark landscape for a place to hide. His blood was pure acid by the time his eyes locked on to a busted sewer grate sticking up like a misshapen metal mouth. He dove inside, and focussed all his mental energy on getting his breathing under control. His heart thundered in his ears and he sucked in huge gulps of dusty air, willing himself to be calm. All he could do now was hope that the hunters didn't see him before he made cover.

As soon as he had his breath under control he realized his mistake. He had chosen the most obvious hiding place. If he were hiding from them and it was the start of the day, he would have been fine, but more than likely he was hiding from one or more tribes. He was now sitting in one of the first places they would look. The best way to evade hunters was to keep moving. So as soon as he got his breath back he started to creep out of the sewer, but it was already too late. He could hear them talking in hushed tones, the harsh whispers echoing in the sewer all around him. He couldn't tell where they were so he had no choice but to stay where he was. He pulled the Glock from his belt, cocked it and laid it in his lap, then he unclipped the shotgun from the concealed cord, pumped it once to chamber a round and waited.

The voices got closer, Jericho had to make a guess as to what side they were coming from. It was 50/50 at this point and all he could do was trust his gut and hope for the best. Bracing his feet against one side of the sewer wall he wedged himself in place, pushing his backpack into the cold concrete curve behind. To his left the sky was a dim pale black, like a moon of waxing gibbous shape, he trained both guns at an angle waiting for the silhouette of a man to appear in front of him. But his guess was wrong and when the shape appeared it was coming from behind him. There was no choice, he had to change his angle and lose the advantage of surprise or take the chance that the silhouette would pass him by. He moved as quietly as haste would allow. The silhouette was armed with a bowie knife, it gleamed in the starlight, but when was a knife ever as good as a gun in close quarters?

He fired both weapons at the same time. The Glock blew a hole in the silhouette's left shoulder, the shotgun tore off most of the dark figure's head. The double boom echoed through the sewer, the second immensely louder than the first. It was like a starter pistol, Jericho was out of the sewer grate and running flat out before the concussive shock could settle into a headache. All he could hear was the high pitched whine as his ear drums vibrated painfully. The dust around him puffed and popped intermittently, someone was taking shots at him as he ran. In the back of his mind his instincts screamed at him. "Snipper, Snipper, take cover damass!" But he had to put distance between him and the hunters so he kept running hoping the shooter had nothing more than a plain old hunting rifle with a bad scope, or better yet no scope. As he ran he zigged and zagged, knowing full well that he was just wasting energy. But he had no clear place to hide, so he scanned his surroundings wildly looking for cover but there was nothing that he thought would hold up against gun fire. His ears were still ringing so he never heard the shot, but he felt it. Like a hand slapping his back knocking the wind out of him. The bullet hit high up on his right shoulder, sending him sprawling in the street.

Jericho pulled himself up painfully. His hands were raw, the burning pain from his scraped off skin hurt more than the shot to his shoulder. But that only lasted a moment. Once his lungs started working correctly, pain blossomed from the bullet hole. "They got me", thought, then the world went black as Jericho passed out from loss of blood.

The air tasted of metal and his mouth was thick and dry like cotton. At first all he could do was try to think past the heavy feeling in his head but then he felt the sharp ache high up on his right shoulder. Someone was digging into his back with something very sharp, it was grinding painfully into the bone and a creaky old woman was talking to herself behind him. "Com'on" the voice cooed as if talking to a baby. "Almost there" it said, and then jubilation. " Gotcha!," the voice exclaimed. The pain in his back lessened somewhat, but it was still close to unbearable. The old woman was cleaning the wound, he knew this because the ache was now replaced by an acute burning sensation caused by whatever she was using as disinfectant.

At some point he must have passed out again, because the next thing he knew he was laying on his side in a bed that felt too small. It was the pain that woke him. He had rolled onto his back for a second and the pain was immediate. The room was dimly lit by a single bulb hanging on a dirty bit of wire that might have been white a very long time ago. The room smelled of old blood and urine. Now that his pain was bearable, his brain allowed itself to think about the situation he found himself in. He was a prisoner that was obvious. But to which tribe was unknown at the moment. All he could do was to hope they were not one of the flesh eaters.

Suddenly it occurred to him that if they were flesh eaters they would not have spent time and resources getting him fixed up. More than likely he would have already been served up as the special of the day. This thought was a brief comfort to him until he started wondering what they were planning. He was contemplating the horror stories he'd heard at the drifter outpost only a few days back. The Neo Romans had brought back the colosseum, gladiator flights designed to ensure death for some unfortunate. He was thinking about how he would manage in a straight fight being good with blades and pistols, but some of the mutts out there were nothing short of monstrous. It was at this moment that he heard an all too familiar voice from somewhere to his left. The voice was sickly sweet with a deep southern drawl, like Scarlet in that movie. " looks like Jericho finally hit a wall." the voice said, and then it laughed at the cleverness of its joke. His blood ran cold in his veins.. "Jackal" he replied softly, "why I am not surprised."

"Oh Come now sugar'" she dragged the words out, teasing each one in turn. "I been looking for you for a long, long time… don't tell me you didn't miss me, Jerry Bear?". "I told you not to call me that." he replied, his tone flat. She was eating an apple and the wet chomping filled out the silence. "I can't says I missed your god awful attitude Jerry Bear" she said around a mouthful of apple, "but I did miss those big brown eyes." He was fully awake now, unsure of what came next, Jackal was unpredictable at the best of times. He ventured a question, an obvious one. "What are you planning to do with me?" She stood, making the metal chair she was setting on, scrap across the ground. "Tell you the truth?... I don't likely know Jerry Bear." He heard a heavy key scrap in the lock and then silence

Jericho sunk back into the mattress. He felt deflated. After years of hard earned freedom, if you could call how he had lived the last few years of his life freedom, he was back with Jaqueline "the Jackal" Mooney. It was his own personal nightmare scenario. When he escaped her particular brand of depravity the first time he had gambled, taking a chance that he would be able to survive the daytime with them. Over the years he got really good at avoiding people. After what Jackal had done to him as a child he had his fill of women. Men were not his thing either so he just stayed away from all people all together. His was a solitary life of a Hunter. He learned to love the night and despise the day. The day time world was ugly, harsh and dusty. Not to mention the unbearable heat. The night was beautiful, maybe because it covered up the ugliness of the real and like all lies, seemed better than the truth because facing the truth was much harder than hiding from it.

And now here he was back in her clutches. He knew she had some punishments planned for him, after all she had years to think about it. His mind was blank as he laid back and resigned himself to his fate. He knew there would be no escape this time. Jackal would make sure of that. The only thing that allowed his escape the last time was the fact that she didn't expect it. She was convinced that he loved her and in a twisted stockholm syndrome kind of way he did, but the abuse was too much for him. Jackal liked hurting him physically and the constant threat of physical pain was causing him mental anguish. She loved him in her own twisted way. It was an unhealthy love, because she was mentally unstable. It's strange what power does to people and when there is nothing to hold the one in power in check, when there are no laws to protect those without power, things get real messy real fast.

Jericho fell asleep again. This time it was a deep sleep, the kind of sleep that comes from knowing exactly where you are, from knowing that for the next few hours you are 100% safe. Nothing was going to get to you, nothing was going to hurt you. Jackal would let him heal before she started her planned torments and until then he was safe from the rest of the world. It was the first time he had slept this deeply in years. It was the sleep of a man that has accepted his fate completely.

The wall vibrated with a hollow boom, boom, boom. Jericho woke, coughing into the dust from the falling plaster. He pulled himself up painfully, swung his legs off the bed and padded barefoot to the door. The concrete was cold and he was weak, but something in the tempo of the booms and the power it had to rattle the entire complex made Jericho very uneasy. He pushed his ear to the door and heard muffled screams. Someone was yelling out orders. He pushed down the urge to call for help knowing that he would get none. But more importantly, if something or someone was attacking the compound it might give him the chance to escape. Gingerly he moved back to the bed, sat down and listened to the rhythmic boom, boom, boom. Now that he was paying attention he became convinced it was them, nothing else on earth was that relentless, or powerful. As the realization took hold his spirit deflated. All thoughts of escape now turned into the hope of survival. But he knew his chances were slim beyond measure. There was no fighting them, all you could do was run. He was trapped and injured. All he could do was sit there and hope that they missed him somehow.

On and on it went. Boom, Boom, Boom… then it stopped. The silence was like an alarm. Jericho went to the door again to listen. He heard muffled gunshots and shrill screaming. They were inside now. It would all be over soon.

His strength was failing him, he felt faint and feverish, but he kept his ear pushed up against the door, desperate to know what was happening outside. It was all a jumble of horrific sounds. Then he felt something or someone slam up against the door. "Fuck he thought" and tried to hold the door closed. If it was one of them he was done for, but if it was a person he had to keep them out if it meant surviving just a little longer. Jericho had never seen one of them, no one ever lived to talk about what they looked like so he had no idea what to expect. The thing on the other side of the door threw itself against the door with decreasing ferocity. It was getting tired, but Jericho was taking no chances and he kept his shoulder firmly planted against the cold metal, with his ear pushed hard into the door, listening intently.

The sounds were dying down, but he remained where he was. There was no point in taking chances at this stage. If it was an attack from another tribe or if it was them, it made no sense to alert them to his presence. It was best to just wait it out. Slowly he slid down the door. The concrete seeped the last remaining warmth from his body, but he stayed where he was propped up against the door like an abandoned marionette. "Safety first" he thought as his body gave in to fatigue. He was woken again by the sound of a key moving in the lock. He forced himself painfully up, pushing with all his strength to keep the door shut. But he was too weak. The door flung open sending him sprawling into the cell.

"Oh Sugar.. I'm so happy they didn't find you" Jackal drawled. She was standing in the doorway, the light from the hall making a silhouette of her. When she moved forward into the cell, Jericho noted her gait immediately, she was hurt. She shuffled over to the bed and dropped into it as if using her last strength to complete the movement. Sighing deeply she eased her legs onto the bed and patted the mattress with her left hand, indicating for Jericho to join her. "Come now Jerry Bear," she pouted. He was still weak so it took some effort but he complied, something in her demeanor told him she was in serious pain. Coming closer he saw her face was pale and drawn, her lips pinched against the pain. Her cheek was smeared with blood and to his shock, she was missing an ear and all the hair on one side of her head.

"They're comin, Sugar… Jerry Bear… I called' em and they came… Can you believe it… They came… hold me" she whispered. "I been fight'n em, Jerry… all's I wanted was to be here with you… So I been fight'n em… so I could get to you, so you could be with me at the end.. They're comin".

Jericho wanted to be mad, this stupid mad bitch just signed his death note. They're coming she had said, that meant the upper levels were overrun and now she had opened the cell and they would come for him. He wanted to hate her, but looking at her sad pent up face, smeared with blood, wisps of gray hair matted to her forehead in tiny curls he remembered how she took care of him as a boy. How she taught him to read and write. She made sure he was fed, and clean and warm… and safe for so many years. Seeing her like this tore a hole in his chest where his heart was supposed to be. The stupid bitch, she killed him by coming here… and she called them? What was she thinking? Then it hit him, she was dying and she was tired of being lonely. She had no one to love, everyone feared her. She was just tired of being alone.

He wasn't mad anymore. She loved him because he was never afraid of her. Warm tears ran down his cheek. Somewhere in the back of his mind he understood that the metallic clicking in the corridor was them, but it didn't matter. He pulled her onto his lap and stroked her hairline on the good side. She looked up at him, her face showed nothing but pent up pain but her eyes radiated love. He looked down on her, her face watery in the tears that were falling freely now. He wondered for a moment if he was crying for her or for his own impending death. Maybe ther were the tears that come from understanding.

It came into the cell, metal sliding over metal, the smell of motor oil and blood filled the enclosed space. Jaqualine looked at it in horror but Jericho kept his eyes on her. He pulled her gaze back to him with the intensity of his eyes. "You look at me", he said. It moved with the sound of gears grinding; there was an awful clicking sound as its limbs scrambled across the concrete. "You look at me", he said. Then there was a wiring sound, and the air hummed for a moment, high pitched like the frenzy of death. Jerricho never felt the blow, the sharp metal blade of its pincer cut through him, and he saw it cut Jacqueline in half with a glorious spray of blood before his consciousness blinked out into the dark void.

38

www.ingramcontent.com/pod-product-compliance
Lightning Source LLC
Chambersburg PA
CBHW050751180726
48003CB00020B/2344